To Mom, Dad, Mara, and Alex,
who have always seen
that I'm more than my Whatifs
—EK

To my loved ones who help me
through my own Whatifs
—ZP

little bee books

New York, NY
Text copyright © 2020 by Emily Galle-From
Illustrations copyright © 2020 by Zoe Persico
All rights reserved, including the right of reproduction in whole or in part in any form.
Manufactured in China TPL 0921
For information about special discounts on bulk purchases,
please contact Little Bee Books at sales@littlebeebooks.com.
First Edition
10 9 8
Library of Congress Cataloging-in-Publication Data is available upon request.
ISBN 978-1-4998-1029-5
littlebeebooks.com

The Whatifs

WRITTEN BY
EMILY KILGORE

ILLUSTRATED BY
ZOE PERSICO

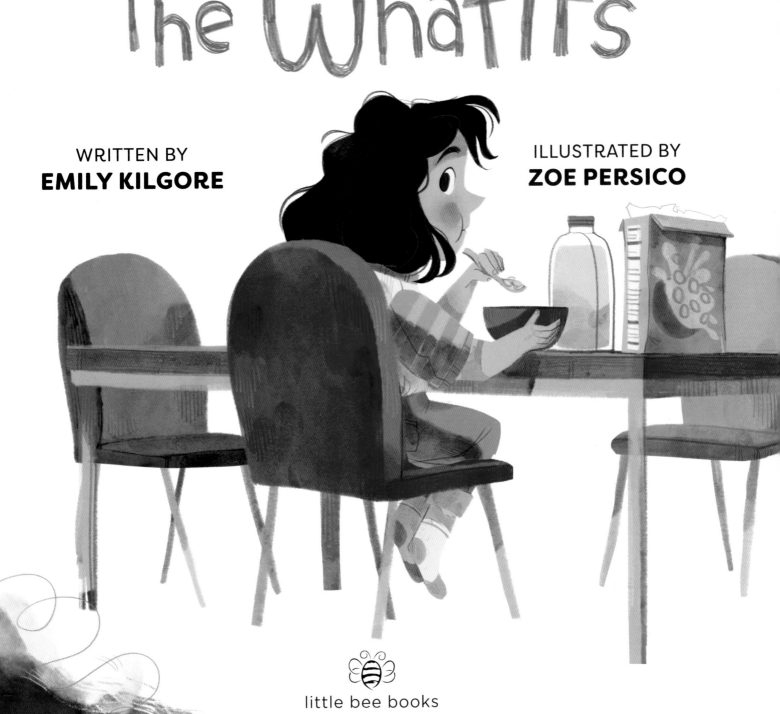

little bee books

Cora was a nervous girl:

always jumpy,
always on edge,
always wondering
if something grim was going to happen.

Because of this, the Whatifs loved her.

Heavy, lumpy, and grumpy, the Whatifs are everywhere:

in bright rooms and dark corners,

in busy hallways and hushed libraries,

in big cities and small towns.

They slink in from unknown places and
swiftly attach themselves to people when they least expect it.

Then they whisper a question
　　so quietly,
　　　　so softly,
　　　　　　so gently,
　　　　　　　　that the person usually doesn't know
　　　　　　　　　　the Whatifs are there at all.

From the moment the sun first peeked through her window in the morning
to the time she pulled a warm quilt over her head at night,
Cora's Whatifs followed her every move.

What if my dog runs away?

What if I forget my homework?

What if the sun stops shining?

What if my crayon breaks?

Many people think about their Whatifs for a moment or two, but can briskly brush them off.

Cora, though, could not.

It didn't matter if the Whatifs' questions were silly or frightening, likely or impossible.

As soon as Cora thought about them, the Whatifs grabbed hold of her.

One week, Cora had more Whatifs than usual.
Her piano recital was just days away.
Even though she had practiced and perfected her song,
the Whatifs started creeping in.

What if my fingers shake?
Cora questioned on Monday.

What if I make a mistake?
Cora wondered on Tuesday.

What if nobody comes?
she thought on Wednesday.

What if too many people come?
she worried on Thursday.

By the day of her recital, the weight of the Whatifs felt unbearable.

Cora stood backstage, anxiously awaiting her turn to perform.

The longer she waited,
the more Whatifs appeared,
each one grabbing hold
and weighing her down
more than the last.

"Cora?" a small voice whispered. "Are you alright?"

Oh, great! Cora thought.
What if Stella thinks I'm a crybaby?
What if she doesn't understand?

"It's nothing" was all Cora could muster before a tiny sob escaped her thinly pressed lips.

"It doesn't sound like nothing," Stella said.

Cora took a deep breath
and said in a hushed voice,

"I . . . I just . . .

I just have too many Whatifs.

They make me imagine bad things that could happen.

Like, *What if I mess up?*

Or *What if I sneeze during my song?*"

"Everybody gets Whatifs, Cora!
Just a minute ago, I asked myself,
What if Cora's sad and I can help?"

Listening to Stella, Cora started to wonder,
   What if she can help me?
   What if I can trust her?

"I wish mine were like that. My Whatifs are grim." Cora looked down.

"Do you ever have good Whatifs?" Stella asked.

"I didn't know there were good ones," Cora whispered.

"Of course there are!" Stella said. "Like,
What if there's chocolate cake after our recital?"

"Or *What if I play better than ever?*" Cora chimed in,
peering at the boy pounding his piece on the piano.

Cora suddenly felt her Whatifs begin to change.

The heavy, lumpy, and grumpy Whatifs slowly slunk away,
while new ones arrived in their place.

Just then, the teacher announced it was Cora's turn.

Cora walked out to the piano without tripping.
The bench was just the right height.
Her hands quivered
as they hovered over
the keys.

But then she sat down and began to play,
and the grim Whatifs slowly continued to disappear until . . .

CLUNK!!!

. . . she hit the wrong note.

Oh, no!
What if everybody laughs at me?
What if I get booed off the stage?
Cora wanted to cry.

She tried to ignore the people staring, waiting for her next move.

Then, out of the corner of her eye, Cora saw Stella.

What if I CAN do this? she asked herself.

Cora took a deep breath and started to play again with confidence.
Her fingers danced across the keys.

When she finished, the room filled with applause.
Cora took her bow and smiled at Stella.

She couldn't help but wonder,
What if . . .

I made a new friend today?

Author's Note

When I was a young child, I was constantly weighed down by anxiety. I feared being away from my family. *What if my parents leave me behind? What if they do something special without me?* And at night, I could not sleep unless the door to my bedroom remained wide open. *What if a monster comes in my room while I'm sleeping?* The muffled voices of my parents talking downstairs was a comfort, and the light from the hallway blanketed my bed. A closed door or dark hall made me feel alone, trapped, scared.

As I grew older, my fear and apprehension shifted. I still battle anxiety—to this day, I dread flying in airplanes!—but what was once frightening is now just uncomfortable. What I understand as an adult is that my anxieties don't make me a lesser person. Even as a young child, I acknowledged that some of my worries were irrational, but I felt powerless to overcome them. I began avoiding sleepovers or spending extended time with friends. I was too bogged down and concerned that nobody would understand. Yet, countless people—young, old, and everyone in between—worry.

According to the Anxiety and Depression Association of America, one in eight children is affected by anxiety disorders. As someone who has experienced anxiety and witnessed it envelop some of my students, I knew *The Whatifs* was a story waiting to be told. In many ways, I am Cora. Many of her "what if" questions were ones I'd asked or heard from my students. Everybody has "what if" questions—they may just ask them in different ways.

With help, support, patience, and hope, these negative Whatifs can be spun around. They can be managed. Like Cora, I've learned to be the boss of my Whatifs. It is with the loving support of my family and friends that I have been able to ask:

What if my journey navigating Whatifs can help others?

What if I CAN write a book?